This book
belongs to:

_____

_____

This edition first published in Great Britain by HarperCollins Publishers Ltd in 2000

1 3 5 7 9 10 8 6 4 2

Copyright © 2000 Enid Blyton Ltd. Enid Blyton's signature mark and the words
"NODDY" and "TOYLAND" are Registered Trade Marks of Enid Blyton Ltd.
For further information on Enid Blyton please contact www.blyton.com

ISBN: 0 00 710637 8

Reproduction by Graphic Studio S.r.l. Verona
Printed in Italy by Garzanti Verga S.r.l.

NODDY IN TOYLAND

Noddy and the Runaway Cakes

Collins

An imprint of HarperCollinsPublishers

It was a beautiful, sunny morning in Toyland.
Bumpy Dog was at Noddy's house helping him
prepare a treat . . .

"This is the perfect day for my tea party with Tessie Bear," said Noddy, as he carefully carried a large plate piled high with cakes. Bumpy Dog jumped up at Noddy to show his agreement.

"Oh, be careful, Bumpy Dog, you almost made me drop these tasty cakes! Now, I'm off to fetch Tessie Bear. You stay here, I won't be very long."

Noddy hummed a happy tune as he drove to
Tessie Bear's house. PARP! PARP! tooted
Noddy's little car.

"The tea party is ready," Noddy called out as Tessie Bear came rushing out of her house. She was wearing her best spotty skirt for the occasion.

"Hello Noddy," she called. "I am looking forward to having tea with you!"

Noddy and Tessie were both really looking forward to eating Noddy's cakes. But when Noddy opened the door . . . Oh, dear, what a shock! There was an empty plate on the table and not a cake in sight, only Bumpy Dog looking very sad.

"Bumpy Dog," said Noddy sorrowfully, "have you eaten all the cakes? I can't believe you'd do such a naughty thing."

Tessie Bear tried hard to cheer Noddy up. She didn't believe that Bumpy Dog would be so naughty.

"Bumpy Dog had a very large lunch today so I don't think he took the cakes, Noddy. But never mind, we can all have honey sandwiches if you take us back to my house."

The next day Noddy set out early to drive Jumbo to Miss Pink Cat's house.

"Oh please hurry up, Noddy," pleaded Jumbo. "Miss Pink Cat has promised to give me some fairy cakes and my tummy is rumbling!"

When they pulled up outside Miss Pink Cat's house she was waiting on her doorstep. Miss Pink Cat was looking very cross indeed!

"It's disgraceful!" she exclaimed crossly. "I went to fetch my teapot from Mr Plod and when I came back all my cakes were gone!"

"Oh, no," wailed Jumbo, "not the fairy cakes," and his tummy gave a sad little rumble.

"Has Bumpy Dog been here this morning?" asked Noddy worriedly.

"Certainly not," said Miss Pink Cat, "but I did see a flash of green. I believe it was Bert Monkey's new jacket."

"Jumbo, I won't charge you for your fare as you haven't had your cakes!" said Noddy kindly. "I am off to look for Bert Monkey now."

Noddy found Bert Monkey sitting at a table in the café, tucking into an iced bun which certainly didn't look like a fairy cake, and he wasn't wearing his new green jacket. As Noddy was thinking about this, Big-Ears rode up on his bicycle, ringing his bell loudly.

"Oh Big-Ears, I am so pleased to see you, we're in such a pickle!" cried Noddy, and he explained all about the missing cakes.

"We must go and see Mr Plod," said Big-Ears firmly when Noddy had finished his tale.

At the police station, Mr Plod was very worried when he heard what had been happening. "Noddy, this is serious. It's my birthday tomorrow and Mrs Tubby Bear is baking a cake. Suppose that is stolen!"

"I might have an idea," suggested Big-Ears, who had been thinking about the missing cakes while Mr Plod had been worrying.

"We'll hold a party at Mr Plod's house, tomorrow at six o'clock.

We can set out all the food before and then we'll
hide and see if we can catch the thief at work."

"That is a good idea, Big-Ears," said Mr
Plod approvingly.

"Let's go and tell the others," agreed Noddy.

The next evening the Toy Town guests arrived for
Mr Plod's birthday party. Tessie Bear brought
apples and oranges; Big-Ears and Noddy came
with a big bag of biscuits; Miss Pink Cat made
sandwiches and Jumbo helped her to carry them.
Milko brought pots of yoghurts and bottles
of milk.

The Tubby Bears carried jellies and a huge birthday cake with blue icing.

"Wait, wait for us," called Bert Monkey. He and Bumpy Dog were the last to arrive. They had brought party hats and balloons. Bert's tail was being very helpful and carrying most of the hats!

When the table was piled high with all the delicious food, everyone hid, chattering excitedly. Jumbo slipped behind the curtains, Big-Ears and Noddy squeezed behind the sofa, Bert Monkey crept beneath the chair and Master Tubby Bear crawled under the table.

"Sssh! It's nearly six o'clock!" announced Mr Plod importantly. Everyone else quickly found somewhere to hide, and the room fell silent.

Moments later the door creaked open and a green arm stretched out towards the big blue birthday cake in the middle of the table. For a second no-one dared to move.

Then, one by one, heads popped out from all the hiding places. Mr Plod made a grab for the green arm and pulled . . .

. . . Sly into the room. With Sly came Gobbo, who had been crouching right behind him.

"Stop! You are under arrest!" called Mr Plod.

It was the naughty goblins who had been taking all the cakes – and Mr Plod had caught them in the act!

"You didn't think you could take MY birthday cake, did you?" Mr Plod boomed. He quickly handcuffed them and then announced . . .

"Now, we can get on with MY party and eat MY special cake."

Everybody cheered and Noddy gave Bumpy Dog a special hug. "I'm sorry, Bumpy Dog. I never really thought it was you. You're the best and most loyal dog anyone could have!"

THE END

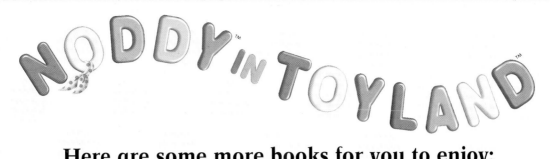

Here are some more books for you to enjoy:

Noddy's Bumper Activity Book
ISBN: 0-00-710640-8

Noddy's Bumper Colouring Book
ISBN: 0-00-710639-4

The Goblins and the Ice Cream
ISBN: 0-00-710786-2

Mr Plod's Bossy Day
ISBN: 0-00-710789-7

Mr Straw's New Cow
ISBN: 0-00-710787-0

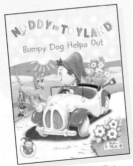

Bumpy Dog Helps Out
ISBN: 0-00-710788-9

Noddy's Special Whistle
ISBN: 0-00-710638-6